THE
ENCHANTER'S SPELL

FIVE FAMOUS TALES

Pictures by Gennady Spirin

· HAMISH HAMILTON · LONDON ·

First published in Great Britain 1987 by
Hamish Hamilton Children's Books
27 Wrights Lane London W8 5TZ

Published in West Germany 1986 as *Spirins Meisterwerke—Nussknacker
und Mausekönig* by Hoch-Verlag, Düsseldorf
Pictures copyright © by Verlag J. F. Schreiber
All rights reserved : Designed by Jane Byers Bierhorst
Printed in West Germany

British Library Cataloguing in Publication Data
The Enchanter's spell
1. Children's stories
808.83′1   PZ5
ISBN 0-241-12320-8

"The Nutcracker" is adapted from the book *The Nutcracker*
by Warren Chappell. Copyright © 1958 by Warren Chappell.
Copyright renewed 1986 by Warren Chappell. Published
by arrangement with Alfred A. Knopf, Inc.

CONTENTS

Little Daylight

One glorious summer morning, there was great rejoicing in the palace of a certain king, for his wife, the queen, had had her first child, and there is as much happiness over a new baby in a palace as in a cottage.

In the great forest next to the palace lived several fairies who always gave a gift to each new baby that came. But there was another fairy who had recently come to the forest, and nobody even knew that she was a fairy except the other fairies. She was a wicked old thing, often being disagreeable in order to tempt people to offend her so that she might take vengeance upon them. She lived in a mud house in a swampy part of the forest.

All the fairies were invited to the baby's christening. But the king and queen never thought of inviting an old witch. The other fairies guarded as well as they could against any harm she might do. But they could not make her powerless, nor could they tell what kind of evil gift she might bring the new baby.

The old witch came without being asked. In fact, not being asked was just what she wanted, so that she might have a reason for doing something wrong.

Five fairies had given the child such gifts as each thought best, when the wicked fairy hobbled up to the archbishop, who, at that moment, was handing the baby to the queen's nurse.

"Please, Your Grace," she said, "I'm very deaf. Would you mind repeating the princess's name?"

"With pleasure, my good woman," said the archbishop, stooping to shout in her ear. "The infant is little Daylight."

"And little Daylight it shall be," cried the fairy in the tone of a dry axle, "and little good shall any of her

gifts do her, for I give her the gift of sleeping all day long, whether she will or not. Ha, ha! He, he! Hi, hi!"

Then a sixth fairy came out. She and the others had planned for her to come after the wicked one, in order to undo as much damage as she could.

"If she sleeps all day," she said, "she shall at least wake all night."

"A nice prospect for her mother and me!" thought the poor king, for they loved their child far too much to turn her over to the nurses as most kings and queens do.

"You spoke before I had finished," said the wicked fairy. "That's against the law. It gives me another chance."

"I beg your pardon," said the other fairies, all together.

"She did. I hadn't finished laughing," said the crone. "I had only got to Hi, hi! and I had to go through Ho, ho! and Hu, hu! So I decree that if she is awake all night, she shall wax and wane with the moon. Ho, ho! Hu, hu!"

But out stepped another fairy, for the good ones had been wise enough to keep two in reserve.

"Until," said the seventh fairy, "a prince comes who shall kiss her without knowing who she is."

The wicked fairy made a horrid noise like an angry cat and hobbled away. She could not pretend that she had not finished her speech this time,

for she had laughed Ho, ho! and Hu, hu!

"I don't know what that means," said the poor king to the seventh fairy.

"Don't be afraid. The meaning will become clear in time," she said.

So the queen prepared for many sleepless nights and after a while the household settled into a routine. At times the palace rang all night with bursts of merry laughter from little Daylight, whose heart the old fairy's curse could not reach. She always dropped asleep at the first hint of dawn. But her merriment was short-lived. When the moon was full, she was in glorious spirits and as beautiful as a child could be. But as the moon waned, she faded, until at last she was wan and withered like the poorest, sickliest child. Then the palace was quiet, for the little creature lay in her cradle, hardly moving. When the first silver thread of the crescent moon appeared, though, she would move her lips and the servants would give her a little food. She would grow better until, for a few days, she was in splendid health. Then, she was always merriest out in the moonlight. Even during her worst times, she seemed better when, on warm nights, they took her cradle out into the light of the waning moon.

As she grew older, she had grown more beautiful, with the sunniest hair and eyes of heavenly blue. But as bad times came on, the change in her was all the more painful. The more beautiful she was in the full moon, the more withered and worn she became as the moon waned. Then she looked like an old woman although her hair and eyes did not change. Her wan face was drawn and wrinkled, and she stooped as if she were eighty years old. At last she had to be put to bed, and there await the flow of the tide of life.

A little way from the palace there was a clearing covered with soft green grass. This was her favorite spot, for here the full moon shone free. Here she had a little rustic house built for her, and she stayed there most of the time. Often, as the moon waned, she would retreat further into the forest, and one night her attendants thought they had lost her altogether. It was morning before they had found her. Feeble though she was, she had wandered into a thicket a long way from the glade, and there she lay fast asleep, of course.

Although the fame of her beauty and sweetness had spread, everyone knew that she was under a bad spell, so no king wanted her for a daughter-in-law.

About this time, in a neighboring

kingdom, a revolution took place upon the death of the old king, and the young prince had to flee for his life, disguised as a peasant. When he got into the land ruled by the princess's father and no longer feared being recognized, he still did not take off his disguise, for he had no other clothes and very little money.

For a day or two he had been walking through the palace forest and had had almost nothing to eat, when he came upon a strange little house, inhabited by a motherly old woman who was, in fact, one of the good fairies.

Although she knew quite well who he was, she said nothing but received him with kindness and gave him bread and milk. She invited him to stay the night, and when he awoke, she would not take any of the money he offered but begged him, if he remained in the neighborhood, to return to her cottage.

"Thank you so much, good mother," answered the prince, "but the sooner I get out of this forest the better."

"I don't know that," said the fairy.

"What do you mean?" asked the prince.

"Why, how should I know?" she replied.

"How strangely you talk!" said the prince.

"Very well," said the fairy.

The prince turned and walked away. The fairy stood at the door of her little house looking after him until the trees hid him entirely. Then she said, "At last!" and went in.

The prince wandered off, but he seemed to come no nearer to the edge of the forest than before. He sat down on a fallen tree, ate a bit of bread the old woman had given him, and waited for the moon to rise. Although he was not much of an astronomer, he knew the moon would come up sometime because it had risen the night before. Up it came, slowly and pretty nearly round.

Again, after walking a considerable distance, the prince thought he was finally coming to the end of the trees. But he found himself only upon the border of a great open space in it, covered with grass. The moon shone very bright, and he thought he had never seen a lovelier spot. He sat down and gazed into the glade. He had not seen so much open space for several days.

All at once he saw something in the middle of the grass—a girl, dressed in white, gleaming in the moonshine. She came nearer and he crept behind a tree, wondering. It must be some strange creature of the woods, a nymph whom the moonlight and the warm, dusky air had enticed from her tree. But when she came close to where he stood, he no longer doubted that she was human—for he had caught sight of her sunny hair and her clear blue eyes, and the loveliest face and form that he had ever seen. All at once she began singing like a nightingale and dancing to her own music, with her eyes ever turned toward the moon. She danced close to where he stood by the edge of the trees, then away in a great circle toward the other side, until he could only see a spot of white on the moonlit grass. She approached again, singing and dancing until she had completed the circle. Just opposite his tree she stood, ceased her song, and broke out into a long, clear laugh, musical as a brook. Then, as if tired, she threw herself on the grass, and lay gazing at the moon. The prince was almost afraid to breathe lest he should startle her, and she should disappear.

She had lain for an hour or longer, when the prince began to wonder about her again. Perhaps she was only a vision of his own fancy. Or was she the spirit of the wood, after all? But she sprang to her feet again, turned her face full to the moon, and began singing as if she would draw it down from the sky by the power of her voice. She looked more beautiful than ever. Again she began dancing to her own music and danced away into the distance. Although the prince watched eagerly, fatigue overcame him and he fell fast asleep. When he awoke it was broad daylight, and the princess was gone.

He dared not leave the glade, and he walked around to see if he could discover any prints of her feet. But the grass was so short, and her steps had been so light, that she had not left a single trace behind her.

He walked halfway around the wood without seeing anything. Then he spied a lovely little house, with a thatched roof and low eaves, surrounded by an exquisite garden, with doves and peacocks walking in it. Of course this must be where the gracious lady who loved the moonlight lived. Forgetting his appearance, he walked toward the door, determined to make inquiries, but as he passed a little pond full of gold and silver fishes, he caught sight of himself, and turned to find the door to the kitchen. There, he knocked and asked for a piece of bread. The good-natured cook brought him in and gave him an excellent breakfast. From her, he learned that this was the favorite retreat of the Princess Daylight. But he learned nothing more, because the cook did not want to be heard talking about her mistress to a peasant lad.

As he rose to leave, he asked the cook if she knew the old woman's cottage. She said she did and gave him full instructions. He left her with many thanks.

Being refreshed now, though, the prince did not go back to the cottage that day. He remained in the forest waiting anxiously for the night, in the hope that

the princess would appear again. Nor was he disappointed, for right after the moon rose, he saw a glimmering shape far across the glade. She was dressed in a pale blue like the sky and looked lovelier still. He did not know that she really *was* more beautiful because the moon was nearer to being full. In fact, the next night the moon would be full, and the princess would then be at the zenith of her loveliness.

At first, the prince feared that she would not come closer that night, but the circles in her dance widened as the moon rose, until at last they embraced the whole glade, and she came still nearer to the trees where he was hiding. He watched the whole night long and saw that as the moon went down, she retreated in smaller and smaller circles, until at last he could see her no more.

Weary as he was, he set out for the old woman's cottage. There he went to bed and slept for many hours. When he awoke the sun was down, and he departed in great anxiety lest he be late. But whether the swamp-fairy had a hand in it or the prince was careless, he lost his way, and the moon was high in the heavens before he finally reached the glade. Then indeed his troubles vanished, for there was the princess dancing toward him in a dress that shone like gold and with shoes that glimmered through the grass like fireflies. She was, of course, even more beautiful than before. Like an embodied sunbeam, she passed him and danced away into the distance.

Before she returned, clouds had begun to gather, and the wind rose and the trees moaned. The prince feared that the princess would go and that he should see her no more that night. But she came dancing on more jubilant than ever, her golden dress and her sunny hair streaming out upon the blast, waving her arms toward the moon, ordering the clouds away from the moon's face. The prince could hardly believe she was not a creature of the elements, after all.

By the time she had completed another circle, there were growlings of distant thunder. Just as she passed the tree where he stood, a flash of lightning blinded him for a moment, and when he saw again, to his horror, the princess lay on the ground. He darted to her, thinking she had been struck. But when she heard him coming, she was on her feet in a moment.

"What do you want!" she asked.

"I beg your pardon. I thought—the lightning—" said the prince, hesitating.

"There is nothing the matter," said the princess rather haughtily.

The poor prince turned and walked towards the wood.

"Come back," said the princess. He obeyed her command and stood before her, waiting.

"I've never seen the sun. Can you tell me what it is like?" she asked.

"No," he answered, "you cannot know what it's like until you see it. It shines like the moon, rises and sets, and is much the same shape as the moon, only it is so bright that you can't look directly at it even for a moment."

"But I would like to look at it," said the princess.

"Why don't you, then?"

"Because I can't. I can't wake. And I never shall wake until—" Here she turned away and walked toward the house. The prince waited a long time, but as she did not come outside again, he set off at last for the old woman's cottage.

It was long past midnight when he reached it, and he went to bed still wondering about the princess.

So far, the swamp-fairy did not know that the prince was in the neighborhood until after he had seen the princess those three times. Now, however, she was going to do all she could. She cast a spell so that the next night the prince could not find his way to the glade. He wandered about the forest until daylight and then fell asleep. The same thing occurred for seven days, during which he also

could not find the old woman's cottage.

After the third quarter of the moon, however, the bad fairy thought there was no chance of the prince wishing to kiss the princess. So on the first day of the fourth quarter of the moon, he did find the cottage, and on the next day he found the glade. For nearly another week he haunted it. But the princess never came. At this period, she always wore a cloak, and there being little or no light, the prince never saw her. Nor would he have known the worn, decrepit creature she now was as the glorious Princess Daylight.

At last, one night when there was no moon at all, he came near the house. There he heard voices. Her women were uneasy because she had slipped out, and no one had seen which way she went. This was a night when she would probably wander very far, deep into the forest. When he understood that she had disappeared, the prince plunged at once into the wood to see if he could find her.

He roamed for hours, and near dawn he came to a great birch tree and sat down wearily at its foot. While he sat he thought to light a fire, which, if she were anywhere near, might attract her. This he managed with a tinderbox which the

good fairy had given him. The fire was just beginning to blaze up when he heard a moan. He sprang to his feet and went around the tree. There lay a human form in a little dark heap. There was light enough from his fire to show that it was not the princess. He lifted it, hardly heavier than a child in his arms, and carried it to the flame. The face was that of an old woman. A hood concealed her hair, and her eyes were closed. He laid her down and took off his coat and wrapped it around her. In a little while she opened her eyes and looked at him—so pitifully! The tears rose and flowed down her gray, wrinkled cheeks, but she never said a word. He begged her to tell him what was the matter, but still she did not speak. He took her in his arms again to carry her to the princess's house, where someone might possibly help her. When he lifted her, the tears flowed yet faster, and she gave such a sad moan that it went to his very heart.

"Poor creature!" he said. "Poor thing!" And he kissed her on the withered lips.

She started, and opened her eyes. But he did not see them, for it was still very dark. Just as he approached the door, she began to move and became so restless that he started to lay her down on the grass. But she stood up on her feet. Her hood had dropped, and her hair fell about her. The first gleam of the morning shone on her face, as bright as the never-aging Dawn, and her eyes were as lovely as the sky of darkest blue. The prince fell back in wonder. It was Daylight herself whom he had brought from the forest! He fell at her feet, not daring to look up until she laid her hand upon his head. He rose then.

"You kissed me when I was an old woman. There! I kiss you when I am a young princess," murmured Daylight. "Is that the sun coming?"

The Princess and the Seven Brothers

On a morning long ago in ancient Russia, the tsar rode off to the wars, leaving his young wife lonely and sad, longing for his return. Each day she sat at the window, but all she saw was the empty plain stretching into the distance. Winter came; snowflakes fell; the plain was covered with snowdrifts. The whole earth seemed to her a vast white emptiness.

Then on Christmas Eve she gave birth to a daughter, and the very next morning, worn with travel, the tsar returned at last. The tsaritsa had double cause for joy! But her time was short. By nightfall she was dead.

The little girl, the tsar's daughter, quiet and gentle, grew to be an amazing beauty, lovely as a flower, with snow-white skin and hair like a raven's wing or a flowing stream at midnight. But it was her charm as much as her looks that made her loved by everyone—no, almost everyone, as you shall see. And when she chose the Prince Yesilei from all her suitors, everyone—that is, almost everyone—rejoiced. The celebrations were arranged; her dowry included seven cities and seven score great mansions, as well as the customary jewels, treasures, and gold.

The tsar had been overcome by grief at the death of his wife. But even a tsar is human, and after a year had passed he had found another wife. You might have thought her a born tsaritsa, tall and slender, fair of face, witty, clever, elegant. But she was also stubborn, jealous, haughty, vain, with a furious temper. Among the rich possessions that she brought with her was a little mirror. Nothing very unusual about that, you might think. But this glass could speak. And since it usually told her what she wanted most to know, it could keep her in good humor when all else failed. Many times a day she would pick it up, put her head on one side, flutter her eyelashes, make a silly pouting mouth, and ask the glass:

Mirror, mirror, tell me true.
Nothing but the truth will do.
You're my friend. You understand.
Who is fairest in the land?

Each time the glass replied:

Queen and friend, my answer take.
I must tell the truth or break.
Lovely ladies are not few,
But none is handsomer than you.

As she heard these pleasing words, the tsaritsa hugged herself; she pranced around with a sideways look and a vain and foolish smile.

On the night before the princess's

wedding, as the tsaritsa studied the clothes that she would wear, she took up the little glass that she had not consulted lately, and spoke to it. But at its response, the tsaritsa leaped to her feet, slapped the little mirror, thumped on the table, and tapped the floor angrily with her heel. "Loathsome thing!" she cried. "What lies you tell! How dare she be my rival, that schoolchild! No wonder she has that horrible white face – her dreary mother had nothing to look at but snow for most of her marriage."

The tsaritsa had asked the same question as she always did. But this time the glass's answer was an unpleasant surprise:

Mirror, mirror, tell me true.
Nothing but the truth will do.
You're my friend. You understand.
Who is fairest in the land?

And the traitorous reply:

Queen and friend, my answer take.
I must tell the truth or break.
All admire your loveliness,
But lovelier is the young princess.

"Tell me, tell me that it was just pretense," said the angry tsaritsa. "Of course, you are joking. Isn't that so?"

But the looking glass had to obey its nature, and again it said:

Queen and friend, my answer take.
I must tell the truth or break.
Wondrous is your loveliness,
But lovelier is the young princess.

This was more than the tsaritsa could endure. Into a cupboard she hurled the glass. She screamed. She swore. Then, breathing hard, she sent for Crow, her maid. "I have a task for you," she said, "and it must be done now. Take the princess into the forest, tie her, head and foot and hand, to a tree, and leave her to be devoured by the first wild creature that passes. Ask no questions. Go!"

Who can argue with a raging woman? So off went Crow, muttering under her breath. It was not hard to persuade the princess to take a walk in the woods, but the rest of the command was another matter. "Not that tree," said the servant to herself. "No, that one won't do either."

On and on they went, and the princess began to feel afraid. Why was Crow mumbling and looking so wild? Had she some orders from the tsaritsa? "Tell me, Crow," she said, "why have you brought me here?"

Then Crow revealed the frightful plan of her mistress. The princess was astonished. "What harm have I ever done to her?" she said. "What harm have I done to anyone? Dear Crow, don't tie me up. Just leave me here to make my way, and when I am tsaritsa you shall have the richest of rewards."

Crow loved the young princess and had no wish to hurt her in any way. "I'll leave you here," she said, "and tell her I've done the deed. Don't sit weeping—look about for a safe shelter; you'll find it, I'm sure of that. God be with you."

And she slowly trudged back to the palace.

"Well? Well?" demanded her mistress. "What happened? Did you do as I said? Do we have any more trouble from the insect, that beetle, that piece of rubbish?"

Crow answered promptly, "She is in the forest, madam, tied securely to a tree. When a hungry wild thing sees her, she won't have time to make a fuss. You can go to sleep and wake in peace."

But through the palace, through the country, whispers and rumors spread. "Where is the tsar's daughter?" "What has become of her?" "Has she been kidnapped?" "Is she dead?" There was one who did not sit idly guessing and that was the Prince Yesilei. Straightaway, he set out to find his vanished bride.

And where was she? Now comes a strange turn to the story. Left alone, the poor girl started walking through the unknown heart of the forest to put as much distance between herself and the palace as she could. But paths were few and there were many trees. Would she ever see bright daylight again? Suddenly she reached a clearing. In the clearing there was a house. From the house a dog ran out. It sniffed at her, stopped barking, wagged its tail, and, looking back as she followed, led her in the friendliest way to the gate. Everywhere, it was so quiet! The door swung open and she stepped inside and climbed the wooden stairs that faced her. At the top was another door. She turned the ring handle and saw before her a long room, warm and inviting. Wooden

benches covered with rugs were all around; the warmth came from a great tiled stove. Clearly, people lived here, but who? Where were they? No one was about. Well, there was no point in being idle. She set to work sweeping the floor, cleaning the pans until they shone, and stoking up the fire. Then, quite tired, she lay down and fell asleep.

Presently she was awakened by loud sounds: horses' hooves, stamping feet, jingling arms and armor. Through the yard and up the stairs, one by one came a

troop of seven young brothers, hunters or, more likely, knights, each one
thick-mustached and handsome. The
first one said, "Now what has happened? Who's been cheering up our
home? Look! A splendid blazing fire!
Shining pans! We *are* in luck. Come

out, wherever you are hiding! If you
are a man, and aged, stay here; you
shall be our uncle. If you are a fine
young fellow, tough as us, and want
adventure, you can join us as a
brother. If you are a kindly dame,
wise in years, we'll call you mother.
And if you are a pretty girl, a fair
young maiden, ah, indeed, you shall
be our own dear sister. We'll all be
glad to serve you."

What could the princess do but
rise and bow to the seven knights? In
a low voice she explained that she had
been lost and seeking shelter when,
by good fortune, she had found this
house. The dog had made her welcome and so she had stepped inside.
Then, to pay for her lodging, she had
cleaned the place.

You may be sure they were all
delighted. They could tell from her
speech and behavior that she was no
ordinary girl, perhaps one of noble
family. But solving that mystery
could wait. They offered her a savory

pie and a glass of wine—they had nothing else to give her—but she asked if she could retire for the night. The best and brightest room was made her own, and there she slept.

And now the princess began to live the happiest of lives. At dawn the brothers would ride out to shoot, to hunt, to battle with Saracens, Tartars, or Circassians, while she, the lady of the house, would set the place in order. At dusk she would welcome them back. Each day brought new words of praise; the hours flew by like gossamer.

All seven grew to love her—how could they help it? At last, they gathered together, and the eldest spoke for the rest. "You know we call you dearest sister. But each of us longs to call you something more. Since you cannot marry all of us, could you think to choose one for your husband? It is bad for us to be rivals instead of friends. Why do you shake your head? Do you reject us all?"

The princess spoke. "Dear brave and handsome brothers, I love you all and each, and your offer does me honor. But I must tell you that I am betrothed already, to the Prince Yes-ilei. On the night before our wedding, an evil being sought my death. I was lured into the forest, escaped the fate that was meant for me, and, wandering I knew not where, I had the great good fortune to find this house and yourselves. No more can I say now."

The eldest bowed low. "Forgive

us, dearest sister. We'll continue as before. That is, if you are willing."

"Indeed I am," said the princess. And all was as it was.

But what now of the tsaritsa? Each time she saw the mirror in the corner of the shelf, her rage returned. One day, however, she felt forgiving. She could have no rival now that the girl was gone. So she took up the glass and, in a wheedling voice, she asked her usual question. The mirror answered:

Queen and friend, my answer take.
I must tell the truth or break.
Your beauty is beyond compare—
Or would be, were not one more fair.
In a wood a maiden dwells
Hers is beauty that excels.

In a terrible voice, the tsaritsa summoned her maid. "Crow by name and crow by nature!" she screeched. "Where is the girl? Tell the truth, there are ways of making you speak!" She learned the story soon enough, and made her plans.

One late afternoon the princess sat at the window, spinning, waiting for

her brothers to return. Suddenly the dog began to bark. An old beggar woman was trying to keep him off with her stick. "Don't be afraid, mother," called the princess. "He is only guarding the house. I'll call him in and you can have a meal."

"Ah, you're a kind one," said the old woman. "But your dog's a monster—he won't leave me alone." That was true. He snarled; the hairs stood up on his back; he continually set himself between the princess and the beggar woman.

"How very odd!" said the princess. "I have never known him to behave like

this. Wait—I will throw you a loaf. It is newly baked; catch it, and have pleasure in eating it."

The woman neatly caught the loaf, thanked the princess, then added, "I have a present for you, too."

She held up an apple, round and ripe. "Enjoy it!" She threw it into the princess's hand and was gone.

The princess looked at the fruit, puzzled. What a curious happening! The dog still seemed upset. She sat down and went back to her spinning. But her gaze kept turning to the tempting gift. Why should she not taste a piece? She lifted the apple and took a small bite. At once her breathing stopped. Her eyes closed; she dropped down limp and cold. The apple rolled along the floor.

At dusk the brothers returned. They were surprised to be met by their dog, who seemed to be urging them to hurry. "What does this mean?" said one knight to another. "An evil omen, maybe." As soon as they opened the door, the dog rushed in, seized the apple, devoured it, and fell dead. It was the brave creature's last loyal act. But a further shock awaited them. Their beloved sister lay in a lifeless heap. They raised her from the bench and wrapped her in as fine a cloth as they possessed, to prepare her for the burial.

Yet what was this? There was still some color in her face, though she breathed not at all. When three days had passed without a change, they decided to lay her in a crystal coffin. This they carried far and far, through lonely plains without a sign of human life, until they came to a high mountain. There, in a large cavern, they suspended their burden by chains from six pillars, so that it gently swayed and did not touch the earth. Then they all stood around the coffin and the eldest spoke solemn words.

"Lie in peace," he said. "Your mortal days were few, but heaven shall have you always. Each of us loved you deeply, but we kept you safe for your own true love. Alas, your bridal bed must be a tomb."

That day the tsaritsa, in a rare good mood, took up her mirror once again and asked the question that it knew so well.

Mirror, mirror, tell me true.
I expect the truth from you.
You're my friend. You understand.
Who is fairest in the land?

Patiently the glass replied:

Queen and friend, my answer take.
I must tell the truth or break.
The prize is yours, I can declare.
None is more lovely; none more fair.

Loudly laughed the tsaritsa in her triumph, and she danced about like a mad thing. "No mortal creature can outwit me!" she cried. "And I'll stand no rivals."

But let us not forget the good Prince Yesilei. Through the land he rides and rides; sometimes he weeps, but the fierce wind blows away his tears. Everywhere he asks and asks: "Have you seen my lost princess? Tell me, tell me, has she passed?" But no one has, and no one tells. Some think him crazy and tap their heads; they laugh behind their hands.

At last, despairing of all humans, he turns towards the Sun. "Great Sun," he calls. "You range the sky. Nothing is hidden from you. I beg you, tell me, have you somewhere seen my lost princess? If you've seen her you will know: hair like midnight, face like snow."

"No, young man, I have not seen her," says the Sun. "Perhaps you should give up the quest unless, of course, she roams the night, a wakeful dreamer of some kind. In that case, try my friend the Moon."

So Yesilei waits restlessly for the day to end. At last, through the violet dark, the Moon began to rise. "O Moon," the young man cried, "you of the silver face and golden horn, who can melt the shadows, have you seen my lost princess?"

The Moon looked troubled. "No, I have not seen the maiden. I have only the nights, you know, and not everyone walks abroad who has a home. But wait— don't look so downcast. Ask my friend the Wind. He may have gone into nooks and crannies, winding places that my light won't travel through. Look him up. I must be moving on. Good-bye."

Yesilei, with beating heart, sought out the Wind's abode. "O Wind, lord of the air, driving the clouds before you, rousing the seas, you who fear nothing at all—except of course the Almighty in his heaven—you won't grudge me an answer, surely? Have you seen my lost princess?"

"I'll tell you this," said the Wind. "Just yonder you will see a trickling stream. Follow it far and far; you will find yourself on a barren plain at the foot of a towering mountain. In the mountain is a cave; in that cave a coffin hangs, a crystal coffin hung by chains. In that coffin lies your bride, who neither sleeps

nor wakes. Unriddle that riddle if you will; I must be on my way." The air was filled with howlings; the Wind had gone.

But Yesilei's eye was caught by the glint of water, a narrow trickling flow. He began to follow it, far and far; and when it vanished at last under the ground, he found himself on a great barren plain from which rose a vast mountain. At its base was a cavern. He stepped inside and in the shadowy half-light, saw a coffin made of glittering crystal, gently swinging from chains. Inside was a girl—yes, his lost princess. Yesilei cast himself on the coffin, murmuring her name. The crystal broke. The maiden sighed, sat up, and looked about in wonder. Then she saw the prince and smiled. He took her hand and led her into the daylight, where they rode away on his horse, telling each other their stories as they went.

Whispers ran through the palace: our princess is alive! She has come home! One who did not hear the news was the tsaritsa, who was sitting in her room, asking the mirror her unchanging question:

Mirror, mirror, tell me true.
Nothing but the truth will do.
You're my friend. You understand.
Who is fairest in the land?

The mirror said:

Queen, Queen, my answer take.
I speak the truth or I must break.
There is one lovelier than you.
The princess lives—it is true.

The tsaritsa leaped to her feet in rage and threw the glass onto the floor. She'd been outwitted after all. It was too much to bear, and that same night she died.

The funeral was soon over, and the guests went merrily on to the marriage feast. For on that day the Prince Yesilei and his princess were wed. The seven knights had been invited, you may be sure, and magnificent they looked as they rode in. They sought no brides for themselves, however, and rode back as they came, since no one could match the princess who had shared their home. Never were there such celebrations, I can tell you, or such a delicious meal. It flowed like the Volga; I know, for I was there.

The Nutcracker

It was Christmas Eve and snow was falling, spreading a soft white blanket over the old city. The sound of sleigh bells and laughter could be heard in the streets, while in the houses there was an air of expectancy as the last preparations were made around the Christmas tree. In Germany it was the custom to give gifts on the night before Christmas, rather than on the day itself.

In the home of Judge Silberhaus, two children waited eagerly outside the closed parlor door. Fritz was a very handsome and willful boy. Marie, his beautiful younger sister, had a gentle, loving disposition.

Few children could look forward to a more exciting Christmas. In addition to the fine presents from their mother and father, there would be those from their godfather, Doctor Drosselmayer, who was no ordinary man. He was tall, thin, and stooped, and in his wrinkled face one eye glowed, while the other was covered by a black patch. On his bald head he wore a wig of spun glass, which he had made himself. He was a remarkable inventor, who was able to make lifelike puppets that walked and danced. Some could even speak a few simple words. A toy cupboard held many wonderful things that Godfather Drosselmayer had made for the two children.

At last the parlor door was opened. And there in the center of the room, the splendid Christmas tree, brilliant with candles, seemed to grow from the table on which it stood. All kinds of toys, goodies, and cookies hung from its branches, and they danced in the twinkling light. More gifts were heaped high around the base of the tree.

Fritz saw a squadron of red-coated

hussars mounted on white horses, which would be a fine addition to his large army of foot soldiers. Then he caught sight of the chestnut horse, which he had wanted most of all. He mounted it happily and galloped about the room.

Marie found a beautiful doll, which she named Claire, and there was also an elegant silk dress. But her attention was quickly caught by a little man made of wood. His body was too long for his thin little legs, and his head was too large for his body. His coat was trimmed with gold braid, and on his head was a green cap. From the back of his neck a piece of wood extended like a narrow cape. His features expressed a gentleness to Marie. His light-green eyes were serene and his smile was cheerful. And he had an engaging curly white beard that covered his chin.

Marie asked her father whom the wooden man belonged to, and he said that it was for both her and Fritz. Her father picked the little man up and lifted his wooden cape. As he did so, the red lips of the figure parted, showing two rows of white teeth. Marie was told to place a nut between the teeth and to press on the cape. The mouth closed as she pressed and the nut was cracked, leaving the kernel in her hand.

Hearing this cracking sound, Fritz left his chestnut horse and begged to crack the next nut. But he pushed such large and hard nuts into the little man's mouth that finally, with a cra-a-ck, the jaw was broken, and several of the small white teeth fell to the floor. Marie burst into tears, and insisted that she alone should have the wounded nutcracker. Godfather Drosselmayer chided her for such devotion to the homely little creature, but Marie's mother and father agreed to put him in her care until he was strong again. Quickly she gathered up the tiny teeth, then tied the nutcracker's jaw together with a ribbon from her new silk dress.

It was late. Godfather Drosselmayer said good night and went out into the snowy street. All the family went off to their rooms except Marie, who begged for a few more moments at the beloved toy cupboard. By the dim light from a ceiling lamp, she tenderly lifted the disabled nutcracker into a soft bed intended for her doll Claire, and, drawing the covers up to his chin, promised to care for him and to ask Godfather Drosselmayer to attend to his loosened teeth and broken chin. At the mention of Drosselmayer's name the nutcracker seemed to wince, and his green eyes glared so brightly that the girl was startled. But he resumed his kind expression so quickly that Marie thought she might have been mistaken, and that the change was caused by the flickering light.

Marie closed the cupboard door and turned to go to her room. As she did so, the big clock, on top of which was a large gilded owl, began to make the purring sound that preceded its striking. Marie saw the owl's wings droop so that they covered the clock, and its catlike face was thrust forward. The clock was striking midnight, and as it struck, the owl took the form of Godfather Drosselmayer, his long coat hanging down where the bird's wings had been.

Then from all sides of the room came a hissing sound. There was a scampering of tiny feet behind the walls, and bright little eyes peered out of the cracks. It was an army of mice, and it advanced toward Marie, rank on rank. Louder and sharper came the hissing, right under her feet. The floor heaved and split and cracked. And the Mouse King, with seven crowned heads, appeared before her.

40

As the army of mice moved toward her, Marie, trembling in fright, fell against a door of the cupboard, shattering the glass, which fell to the floor with a crash. She felt a sharp pain in her arm. At the noise of the crash, the mice disappeared into the cracks in the walls again.

Now a commotion began in the cupboard. The toys were sounding a call to battle. Nutcracker threw back the covers and sprang out of bed. As he did so, the hissing began again, and the Mouse King and his army came out of hiding.

Nutcracker jumped from the upper shelf, drew his sword, and took command of his army of toys. Drums beat, trumpets sounded, and the little army descended from the cupboard shelves. They were a brave band, but they were no match for an endless horde of mice. Nutcracker was forced back again and again, until he was at the base of the cupboard. Marie could bear the sight no longer. She took off one of her shoes and hurled it into the midst of the battle, striking the Mouse King, and rolling him over on the floor.

At once all the fighters disappeared—the mice into the walls, the toys into the cupboard; again Marie felt the sharp pain in her arm. She tried to reach a chair, but before she could do so, she fainted away.

Sunlight was streaming through the frosted windowpanes of her room when

Marie awoke. Her mother and the doctor were bending over her bed anxiously. She asked about Nutcracker and wanted to know whether the mice had gone away. Although she described the battle between the toys and the mice, she could see that neither her mother nor the doctor believed her story. They said soothingly that she must rest, that the mice had gone away, and that the little nutcracker was back in the cupboard, happy and well.

The next evening Godfather Drosselmayer came to see Marie. He sat beside her bed, and told her a story to explain how Nutcracker and the Mouse King had become enemies.

In a small country, not far from Germany, a beautiful baby girl was born to the king and queen. Her hair was long and golden, and her teeth pearly white. The king and queen named her Pirlipate.

The queen said Pirlipate must be guarded all of the time, so she was watched over by six strong nursemaids who sat around the cradle, each with a cat on her lap. These unusual measures were taken because of Dame Souriconne, the Mouse Queen. Many months before the princess was born, the Mouse Queen had vowed to cast a spell on the firstborn of the royal couple.

This was all because the king was very fond of sausages. When the court astrologer told him the time was right for sausage-making, he asked the queen to prepare them in the way she had always done. While the queen was in the kitchen cooking a large quantity of pork for the king's favorite dish, Dame Souriconne appeared from her home beneath the hearth. She begged for some of the meat. Out of kindness, the queen gave her a juicy morsel. But the delicious odor attracted the Mouse Queen's seven sons and numerous relatives, who greedily fell upon more of the pork. This commotion brought servants running with brooms and brushes, and the mice were soon driven back under the hearth. The loss of so much good meat ruined the quality of the queen's sausages. This made the king so angry that he decided to put an end to the mice.

He sent to Germany for the famous inventor Drosselmayer, who on arriving at the palace was told to devise some means of getting rid of all the mice there. The inventor set to work at building a hundred little oblong boxes, each with a wire inside, to which a piece of salt pork was attached. When the meat was removed from the wire, a tiny door would close behind the thief, shutting him in. With these boxes, all the mice in the palace were caught—all, that is, except Dame Souriconne, who was much too clever to be taken in by such a simple scheme. And although the inventor was sent away with a handsome reward, he did not know that his work was not finished. The Dame lived, and she appeared soon after to the queen and threatened to cast a spell on the queen's firstborn child.

The threat was accomplished. One night, when the princess was only three months old, the six guardian nursemaids, each with a cat on her lap, fell asleep.

Dame Souriconne had been waiting for this moment to carry out her dreadful plan. One of the nursemaids awoke just in time to see the mouse leaving the princess's cradle, and she sounded an alarm. The child was crying, she was alive. But when the nursemaids looked at Pirlipate, they saw that her eyes had become bright green, her mouth reached from ear to ear, her head was too large for her body, and a small white woolly beard was on her chin.

Again Inventor Drosselmayer was sent for. This time he was told that he must break the spell or lose his head. His assignment seemed impossible because the inventor had but one small clue to help him: the princess had become very fond of nuts. By consulting the court astrologer, who in turn consulted the stars, Inventor Drosselmayer found that in order to break the spell Pirlipate must eat the

kernel of the nut Krakatuk. The shell of this nut, so hard that a cannon's wheel could run over it without crushing it, must be broken in the presence of the young princess by a young man who had never been shaved and always wore boots. The kernel of the nut must be presented by the young man with his eyes closed, after which he was to *take seven steps backward without stumbling.*

The king told Inventor Drosselmayer and the astrologer to search for the nut Krakatuk and for the young man who could crack it. So they set out, and for fourteen years and five months they searched the world over, without success. Finally, though it meant death, the inventor knew there was nothing to do but go back to the king and admit his failure.

Because he returned faithfully, Drosselmayer was spared death, but was sentenced to prison for the rest of his life. He begged only that he be allowed to return to Germany for a brief visit with his brother, a toy merchant. The favor was granted to him. Accompanied by the astrologer, Inventor Drosselmayer hastened to the home of his brother, to whom he described his adventures and explained his troubles.

When the nut was mentioned, Brother Drosselmayer remembered that he himself possessed a nut that might be Krakatuk. He fetched a box in which lay a large gilded nut. With great delight the three men discovered KRAKATUK carved on its shell in Chinese characters.

While they were rejoicing in the discovery of Krakatuk, the toy merchant's son, Nathaniel Drosselmayer, a handsome young man of eighteen, came into the room, and there was a happy reunion between him and his uncle, the inventor. The astrologer studied this young man intently, and after asking him some questions, he learned that Nathaniel always wore boots, that the hairs on his chin had never been shaved, and that his hobby was cracking nuts. Indeed, his nickname was Nutcracker. This surely was the young man the stars had predicted would be able to crack the nut Krakatuk!

After a piece of wood was fastened at the back of his neck in order to

strengthen his jaw, Nathaniel was dressed in costly new clothes. Then, with his uncle and the astrologer, he went back to the little kingdom where Pirlipate waited to be rescued from Dame Souriconne's spell.

Many young men came forward, hoping to succeed in cracking the nut. All of them failed in their attempts, but Princess Pirlipate secretly hoped that the handsome Nathaniel, who was the last to try, would be successful. She was over-joyed when he easily crushed the thick shell between his teeth. As she ate the kernel of Krakatuk, she became, once more, angelically beautiful.

But when Nathaniel, blindfolded, took the seven steps backward, the Mouse Queen burst through the floor and threw herself under his feet.

Nathaniel's heel came down on her; he stumbled, and, alas, the handsome young man became as deformed and ugly as the princess had been.

Instead of winning the princess he was ordered from her presence and, along with his uncle and the astrologer, he was banished from the kingdom.

At nightfall the astrologer consulted the heavens once more, and the stars foretold that young Drosselmayer, now a nutcracker, might still become a prince if he wished to be one. He could make his choice when his deformity disappeared. But it would vanish only after he had overcome the Mouse King with seven heads, who was the son and heir of Dame Souriconne; and after he had won the love of a charming young lady—in spite of his ugliness.

When Marie was allowed to get up, she went straight to the glass-doored cupboard. Nutcracker was completely restored, and with all his teeth in place. Gazing at him, Marie was sure that he must be the bewitched nephew of Inventor Drosselmayer, who was none other than her own godfather. She spoke to Nutcracker softly, offering him her loyalty and affection. In return, the little man appeared to reply to her, asking her help and pledging himself to be faithful to her too.

That night Marie was awakened by the hissing sound that she remembered so well, and then she saw the Mouse King standing by her bed. He demanded that she give him her sugar-plums and marzipan, or he would kill Nutcracker. The girl gave him the sweets. The next night the seven-headed creature came again, ordering her to surrender her china figurines to him if she wanted to save her friend. A third night he came, and it was her picture books that she had to sacrifice.

Marie finally told the nutcracker about the Mouse King's greedy demands. At that, Nutcracker's mouth moved jerkily, and he said she must not give up anything else. If she would find him a strong sword he would take care of their enemy. From her brother, Fritz, she borrowed a toy sword and gave it to Nutcracker.

Too excited to sleep that night, Marie heard the clock strike twelve. At the final stroke, noises came from the parlor. There was a clinking of swords, a scurry of tiny feet—then silence. Presently she heard a soft knock at her door. She swiftly opened it and there stood Nutcracker, sword in hand.

He beckoned to Marie to follow him. Together they went to a closet in the hall. From a sleeve of one of

Judge Silberhaus's coats Nutcracker pulled down a little stairway. They had no sooner set foot upon the stairs than they were transported down to a perfumed meadow, which glittered and gleamed as if it were strewn with precious stones.

It was the Meadow of Sugar Candy. Nutcracker led Marie through a splendid door made of orange-flower jam, pralines, and raisins. They journeyed on and came to the Christmas Forest, in which the trees were covered with snow and lit with thousands of candles. Others were hung with fruits of many colors.

Nutcracker clapped his hands, and shepherds and shepherdesses, hunters and huntresses came out of the forest. A ballet was performed to the music of reed pipes and hunting horns. When it was over, the little group of dancers vanished into a thicket.

Marie and Nutcracker walked on past the Orange River, and came to the River of the Essence of Roses. Again Nutcracker clapped his hands, and a swan-shaped boat appeared, made of shells and drawn by golden dolphins.

In this boat they crossed to the City of Jam. Its ramparts and towers were built of glacé fruits covered with crystallized sugar. As they entered the gate to the city, soldiers of silver saluted them and a little man in a gold brocaded coat embraced Nutcracker and welcomed him to the City of Jam.

Delightful little people dressed in gaily colored clothes filled the streets. The dazzling palace that faced the square was called the Palace of Marzipan. Four beautiful little ladies came out from the palace to greet Nutcracker; they called him Prince and Brother. They were princesses of the City of Jam, and when Nutcracker told them Marie had once saved him by throwing her shoe at the Mouse King, the princesses hailed her as the rescuer of their brother.

Marie felt herself being enveloped in a soft mist. Sounds grew dimmer and dimmer; she was rising higher and higher. Suddenly she fell, as if from a great height, and woke up. It was daylight, and she was in her own bed.

Marie did not tell her family about all the wonderful things that filled her imagination. But as the years went by, she grew into a quiet, charming girl, so absorbed in her thoughts that she was often called a dreamer.

One day near her sixteenth birthday, Marie was in the parlor near the toy cupboard, and she began to speak to Nutcracker. She told him she would never have treated him as the Princess Pirlipate had done, because she loved him too well.

As she spoke the word love, Marie heard a step, and looking toward the parlor

door she saw a handsome young man carrying a bouquet, which he presented to her. The young man was Godfather Drosselmayer's nephew, Nathaniel.

At dinner young Drosselmayer obligingly cracked nuts for everyone, and afterward he asked Marie to go with him into the parlor where the toy cupboard stood. There he asked for her hand, and told her that together they would reign over the Kingdom of Toys and Sugar Candy.

The judge and his wife gave their consent to the marriage, provided that the young couple would wait a year. And Godfather Drosselmayer gave his blessing. Marie and Nathaniel were married in the Palace of Marzipan. And in that beautiful country where Marie still reigns with the Nutcracker King, there are as many wonders as ever for those who have eyes to discover them.

The Beautiful Kitchen Maid

Two gentlemen, Don Diego de Carriazo and Don Juan de Avendaño, once lived in the city of Burgos and this story is the tale of their two sons, who were friends from childhood.

When young Carriazo (whose name was also Diego) was thirteen, he left home to go adventuring. He traveled all over his native land of Spain and made friends wherever he went. Best of all, he liked the tuna fisheries of Zahara in the province of Cadiz, where all the rogues and vagabonds of Spain gather once a year and lead a wild, merry life.

Diego spent three summers with his carefree companions at the tuna fisheries and then decided to go back to Burgos, since he missed his father and mother very much and longed to see them again.

They were delighted to see their missing son come home safe and sound. And there were many tales to be told, but Diego was careful not to mention the tuna fisheries, except to his childhood friend, young Tomás de Avendaño. To Tomás he described the simple life of a fisherman in such glowing terms that they soon decided to spend the next summer in Zahara together.

So when the time came they set out—not for the university at Salamanca, where their fathers thought they were going—but for the tuna fisheries, with their pockets well lined with money intended for their studies, which they planned to spend freely, with their merry companions instead.

But that was not to be.

A few days' journey from home, when they were in Toledo, they heard two mule drivers talking about a cer-

tain girl and praising her beauty.

"She is only a kitchen maid at the inn called The Sevillian," they said, "but she has the loveliest face in the world, and she is as good as she is beautiful."

The curiosity of the two friends was aroused, so they went to stay at the inn the mule drivers had mentioned, hoping to see this beautiful girl. They had to wait for a long time that evening, but at last a door opened and in came a girl of about fifteen, wearing a dark green peasant dress.

Tomás, especially, was thoroughly enchanted by the grace of her movements, her delicate figure, and her beautiful, wavy red-blond hair, which framed her head like the purest gold. He looked into her face and fell in love with her eyes and her smile, which might have been painted by the angels. So there he stood, spellbound, gazing at her until she went out again.

The next morning Tomás offered to work for the innkeeper, and he was taken on as a groom to care for the horses. Diego found work at the inn too, as a water carrier, so now they could both be near to the beautiful kitchen maid, whose name was Constanza.

The next day while Tomás went about his work at the inn, yearning to

see Constanza again, Diego went off to carry water.

However, he was out of luck that morning. His donkey picked a fight with the donkey of another water carrier, an old man. The very stubborn creatures fiercely butted each other until the old water carrier's donkey fell to the ground exhausted, breaking the jars it was carrying, and the precious water splashed about both donkeys' ears.

The old water carrier, being the injured party, seized young Diego by the collar and started beating him, so that Diego was forced to shake the old man off quite roughly, reluctant though he was to do so. The old water carrier fell and struck his head on a stone. He lay on the ground, looking as if he were dead.

Diego turned pale as a sheet. Had he killed a man? He was about to go to the old water carrier's aid when he found himself surrounded by other carriers from all over the town, who dragged him before the magistrate with many kicks and blows. The end of it was that Diego was sent to prison, while the injured man was taken to the hospital.

The innkeeper was deeply angry when he heard the story. But Tomás calmed him, and out of the money the two friends had brought with them, gave him a generous sum to compensate him for his loss.

Now an anxious time followed. It was three weeks before the old man recovered and Diego was let out of prison, to his great relief. All was well again! He asked Tomás for news of the beautiful kitchen maid.

"She is hardly a kitchen maid," said his friend. "All she does is look after the silverware here."

"Then why does the whole town call her the beautiful kitchen maid if she washes no dishes?" asked Diego.

"Perhaps it's because she cleans silver instead of scouring iron pots and earthenware platters," said Tomás. However, he had to admit that he had not come to know the shy girl any better in all this time, although not an hour had passed that he hadn't thought longingly of her.

So next day, as he was working, he made up some lines of poetry and wrote them down in his notebook, meaning to copy them out again later:

Who may Love's joys discover?
The silent lover.
To what is Love inclined?
A steadfast mind.
To win Love, what's the art?
A faithful heart.
So may I hope to prove
Devotion to that pearl
Constanza, my sweet girl,
By silent, steadfast, faithful love.

58

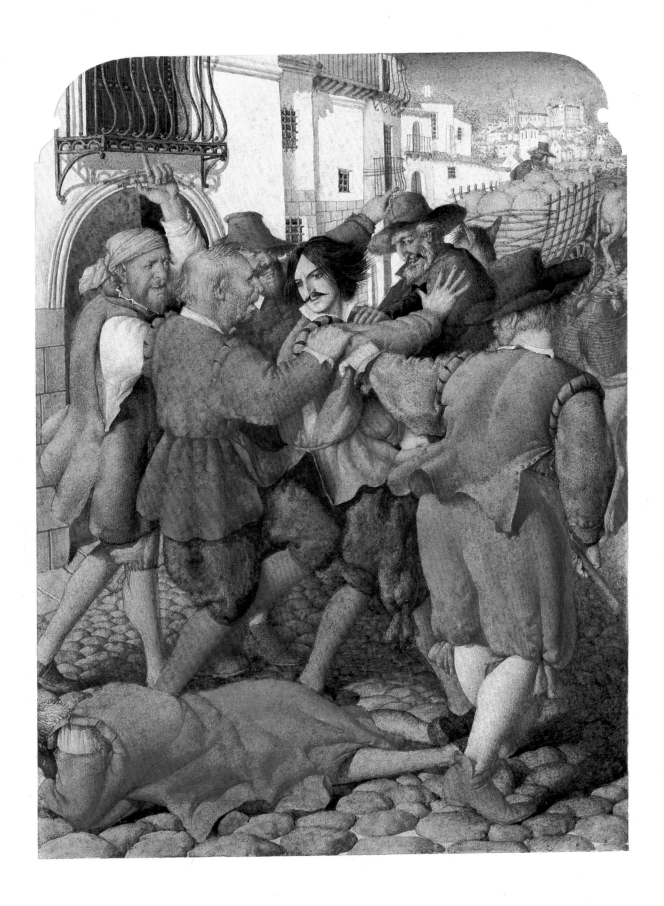

But before Tomás could copy the lines out and then erase them from his notebook as he had planned, they fell into the hands of the innkeeper, who at once asked Constanza what this meant. Not that there was much she could tell him, and she assured him that Tomás had never approached her, never even spoken to her.

So the innkeeper and his wife decided to let the young man go on working at the inn. After all, they thought, he might have written those lines with some other Constanza in mind.

The beautiful Constanza herself, however, was not displeased with young Tomás's poem.

The very next day, he found an opportunity to speak to her when she came

into the main room of the inn with a thick scarf wrapped around her head. When Tomás asked what the matter was, she said she had a toothache.

"Señorita Constanza," said Tomás, seizing his chance, "I will write you down a prayer which, if it is recited twice, is a sure cure for the toothache!" And he hastily wrote down the following lines and slipped them into Constanza's hand:

"Lady of my heart! I am a nobleman of Burgos, rich enough to make you happy all of your days if you will be my wife. The fame of your beauty brought me here to be near you, disguised as a servant. Only tell me what proof of devotion to give you, for I love you more than my life! And I beg you, don't betray me, since I would surely die without you."

He then waited anxiously for her answer, which was not long in coming.

Tearing his note into shreds, Constanza said, "Tomás, this sounds to me more like some kind of magic charm than a holy prayer! I have torn it up in case any other innocent girl should set eyes on it!" So saying, she went out of the room, leaving Tomás with mixed feelings.

He thought perhaps she liked him too, since she had not given him away and had been careful to remove all trace of his approach to her.

However, Tomás had no time for such thoughts at that moment, because the *corregidor*, the mayor of the town, whose son was also in love with Constanza, arrived at the inn with a great many followers, asking to speak to the innkeeper privately.

"I am told there is a kitchen maid of wonderful beauty living here," said the *corregidor*, when he was alone with the innkeeper. "My son has fallen in love with her, and I would like to see her for myself."

So Constanza was sent for. The *corregidor* was delighted with her, and praised his son's good taste. "Landlord," said he, "it is not right for such an angelic creature to live here as your maidservant. In the future, she must think of me as her father, and I will look after her."

However, the innkeeper said he could not agree to that and added that there was a secret he must now tell the *corregidor* about the strange circumstances of Constanza's birth.

"Constanza neither is nor is not my maidservant," he began mysteriously. "Let me tell you how this dear child came to our house.

"Fifteen years, one month, and four days ago a noble lady dressed as a pilgrim and carried in a litter came here with a fine retinue. I would have said she was about forty years old, and she was dazzlingly beautiful, though she seemed rather tired. She immediately sent for the best doctor in town, and he told us to have a bed made up for her in the farthest corner of the house. No one but her maid was allowed to enter this room and wait on her.

"We had been wondering what all this might mean when, making us swear a solemn vow of silence, the noble lady told us that she was very soon going to have a baby. However, she said, no one was to know; so that she could bear her child in secret, she had said she was going on a pilgrimage because she had the dropsy, and the swelling of her body seemed to bear her story out.

"Soon after the noble lady's arrival at our house Constanza was born, and her mother gave my wife, whom she had come to trust completely, several hundred golden coins, asking my wife to look after the baby for a little while. The lady said she would send for her child as soon as she could.

"Then she wrote something down on a piece of parchment and tore it in half, broke several links off a golden chain, and gave half the chain and half the parchment to me, taking the other halves away with her. One day, she said, she would give them to her messenger, and he would show them when he came for the child.

"Then she left, in tears, and went on with her supposed pilgrimage. But no messenger ever came back for the baby. So ever since, we have brought up the noble lady's child as best we could, and you can see for yourself how beautiful Constanza has turned out to be."

The innkeeper ended his story, and it so surprised the *corregidor* that it was some moments before he could reply. And now everything seemed to happen all at once, for two old noblemen of distinguished appearance, accompanied by four horsemen, arrived at the inn and came in.

Tomás, who had come running to see to the guests' horses, immediately recognized his own father and Diego's.

He was much alarmed, thinking that the two old gentlemen must have followed him and Diego here to punish them for their disobedience. So he ran off to hide.

Meanwhile, the two noblemen now politely introduced themselves to the innkeeper, saying their names were Don Diego de Carriazo and Don Juan de Avendaño.

Next they told him why they had come, and now there was no end to everyone's wonder and amazement! For Don Diego took several links of chain out of his pocket, with half a piece of parchment, and the halves fitted the chain and the parchment still in the landlord's keeping so well that there could be no doubt that these were the mysterious lady's tokens.

The rejoicing was even greater when Don Juan de Avendaño recognized the *corregidor* as a dear old friend of his.

Then Constanza herself was summoned, and she too was amazed, and in great confusion.

By now everyone wanted to know the true secret of her birth, and Don Diego de Carriazo began to tell the following tale:

"I am your father," he solemnly told Constanza, "and I am sorry to tell you that your mother is dead. I will say only that she was a lady of the highest rank. I met her by chance, and came to love her. However, we could not marry, as I already had a wife, and so, in tears, we had to part.

Two years later I learned that she had died, but I never guessed she had a daughter.

"A short time ago I heard from her old steward, now on his deathbed. He gave me the tokens and told me of my child. He also relinquished the gold which his mistress had left as a dowry for her daughter and admitted that greed had prevented him from telling me everything at the time of her death. So I rode straight here immediately to try and find our child."

And Don Diego took Constanza lovingly in his arms.

No sooner had Don Diego finished his tale than young Diego came in. Don Diego was much surprised to see his son. Then Tomás too was summoned, and though the fathers said a few stern words to their sons, the joy of their meeting soon outweighed everything else.

Tomás confessed to his father that his love for Constanza had kept both young men at the inn.

That night, the whole party was invited to a sumptuous feast by the *corregidor*. And it was quickly settled that Tomás was to marry the lovely Constanza. As for Diego, before long he fell in love with one of the *corregidor*'s daughters, so a magnificent double wedding was celebrated that summer.

The newly weds stayed on in Toledo for a month. The story of Constanza and the two young men had spread fast in the city. Many people came to see them, especially to admire Constanza's beauty.

When they returned to Burgos, the young couples often met, and liked to look back to the days when Don Carriazo worked as a water carrier, and Don Avendaño as a groom, and they had wooed Doña Constanza, the beautiful kitchen maid.

The Emperor's New Clothes

Many years ago there lived an emperor who was so fond of fine clothes that he spent all his money on dressing in the latest fashions. He wasn't interested in his army and he didn't care for the theater or even for going out for a drive in the park, unless it was to show off his new clothes.

He had a new coat for every hour of the day, and just as people often say about a king that "he's in his council chambers," so in this country they always said, "The emperor is in his dressing room."

In the great city where he dwelled, life was enormously pleasant and many strangers traveled through it every day. Then one day, two very clever swindlers arrived.

They told people that they were weavers and said that they knew how to make the loveliest cloth that you could possibly imagine. Not only were the colors and patterns astonishingly beautiful, they said, but clothes that were made from the cloth had the strange characteristic of being invisible to anyone who either was unfit for his job or else was extremely stupid.

"Those must be excellent clothes," thought the emperor. "If I wore them, I would know which people in my kingdom weren't doing their jobs properly. I could tell clever people from stupid ones. I must have some of that cloth woven for me right away."

The emperor gave the swindlers a lot of money so that they could begin their work at once. The men set up their loom and pretended to be hard at work, even though there was absolutely nothing on the loom. Then they demanded the finest of silks and gold threads, which they immediately stuffed into their own baggage, and they worked away at the bare loom until late at night.

"I *would* like to know how they are getting on with their weaving," thought the emperor. But to tell the truth, he was a little uneasy when he remembered what the two men had said—that anyone who was stupid or unsuited to his post couldn't see the cloth. Of course, the emperor was confident that he needn't be afraid for

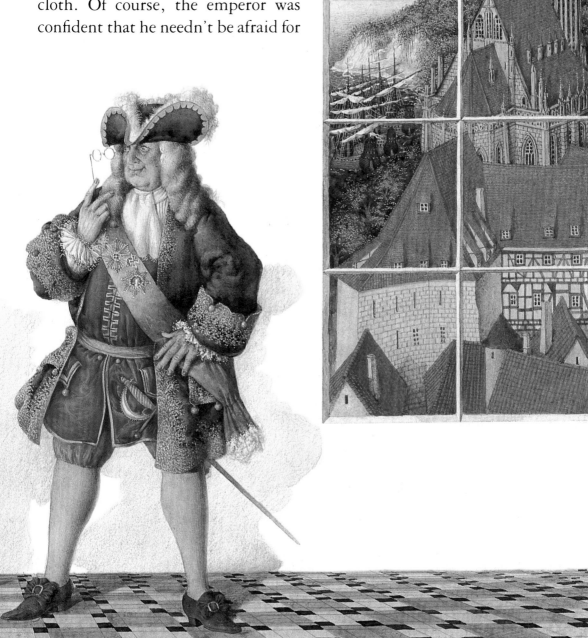

himself. All the same, he decided to send someone else first to see how things were coming along. Everyone in the whole city knew what marvelous powers the cloth had, and everybody wanted to see how incompetent or stupid their neighbors were.

"I'll send my good old minister down to the weavers," thought the emperor. "He can easily see how the stuff is shaping up. He's an intelligent man, and no one is better fitted for his post than he is."

So the worthy old minister went into the hall where the two swindlers were sitting, working at the bare loom. "Heaven help us," thought the old minister, staring with his eyes wide open. "I can't see a thing." But he didn't say so.

Both the swindlers begged him to come closer and asked him if he didn't think it was a pretty pattern with beautiful colors. They pointed to the empty loom, and the poor old minister kept staring at it, but he couldn't see anything, of course, because there was nothing to be seen. "Goodness gracious," he thought, "can I be stupid? I never thought so, and nobody must find out. Can I be unfit for my job? No, no! I can't possibly say I can't see the cloth."

"Well, what do you think of it?" asked the swindler who was weaving.

"Oh, it's charming! Most delightful!" said the old minister, looking through his spectacles. "The pattern! The colors! Yes, I must tell the emperor that I am extremely pleased with it."

"We are glad indeed to hear it," said both the weavers, who proceeded to name the colors and describe the unusual pattern. The old minister listened carefully so as to be able to repeat it when he went back to the emperor, and so he did. The swindlers now demanded more money and more silk and gold thread to be used in the weaving. They pocketed it all; not a thread was put on the loom, but they went on weaving as before.

Very soon, the emperor sent another honest official over to see how the weaving was progressing and whether the cloth would be ready soon. The official fared as the first minister had. He looked and looked, but as there was nothing there but the empty loom, he couldn't see anything.

"Well, isn't that a fine piece of cloth?" asked both the swindlers, pretending to show the material and explain the lovely patterns that weren't there at all.

"I am not stupid," thought the man. "Is it that I'm unfit for my fine job? That wouldn't be very funny! But I mustn't let people suspect anything." So he praised the cloth which he couldn't see and assured the two men that he was pleased with the beautiful colors and the lovely pattern. "Yes, it is exquisite,"

he told the emperor. "Everybody in the city is talking about the wonderful cloth."

Finally, the emperor decided to go and see it himself while it was still on the loom. He brought with him his most important friends and cabinet ministers—including the two worthy officials who had been there before. He went to the hall where the two clever swindlers were now weaving with all their might, still without a vestige of a thread.

"Now, isn't that magnificent?" said both the worthy officials. "Will Your Majesty observe the beauty of the design and the unusual colors?" And they pointed to the bare loom, for they each supposed that all the others could certainly see the cloth.

"What's the meaning of this?" thought the emperor. "I can't see a thing! This is terrible! Am I stupid? Am I not fit to be emperor? That would be the most awful thing that could happen to me."

"Oh, it's very pretty, it has my utmost approval!" he said, nodding confidently and gazing at the empty loom. Of course he wouldn't say that he could see nothing.

All of his friends and ministers looked and looked, but they saw no more than the emperor had. However, they hastily agreed with the emperor, saying wisely, "Oh, it's truly

lovely!" And they advised him to wear clothes made from the splendid new material on the occasion of a great procession which was to take place shortly.

"Magnificent! Exquisite! Excellent!" they exclaimed. They all seemed to be thrilled at what they saw. The emperor presented each of the swindlers with a medal and a knight's cross to wear in his buttonhole, and he also gave each one the title Gentleman of Weaving.

The swindlers sat up the whole night before the day when the procession was to take place, and they had sixteen candles lit in their workroom. People could

see that they labored well into the night to finish the emperor's new clothes.

They pretended to be taking the cloth off the loom, they clipped with scissors in the air, they sewed with needles without thread—and finally they announced, "At last! The emperor's clothes are ready." The emperor, along with the noblest of his personal attendants, came forward. Each of the swindlers

raised an arm in the air as if holding something up, and said, "See, here are the stockings, this is the coat, this is the mantle," and so on. "It is as light as a spider's web, so you would think you had nothing whatever on, but that, of course, is the beauty of it."

"Yes," said all the emperor's attendants. But they couldn't see anything, for there was nothing to be seen.

"Will Your Imperial Majesty please take off your clothes?" said the swindlers. "We can then put the new ones on you here, before the large mirror."

The emperor took off all his clothes, and the swindlers acted as if they were handing him each piece of the new suit which was supposed to have been made. They put their hands about his waist and pretended to tie something securely. It was the train, part of the royal robes, which flowed behind as he walked. The emperor turned and twisted in front of the glass.

"How well it fits! How beautifully it suits him," they all cried. "The

pattern and the colors! It is indeed a noble costume!"

"The people are waiting outside with the canopy which is to be carried over Your Majesty in the procession," said the master of ceremonies.

"Very well, I am ready," said the

emperor. "Doesn't it fit well?" Once
more he turned about in front of the
mirror, admiring his new finery. The
lords-in-waiting, who were to carry
the train, fumbled a bit, as if they
were picking it up. They walked on,
holding the air—for they too didn't
want to let it be known that they
couldn't see anything at all.

So the emperor walked in the procession under the beautiful canopy, and everybody said, "How splendid the emperor's new clothes are! How beautifully they fit!" No one wanted to be discovered seeing nothing, for that would mean that they were no good at their job, or that they were very stupid.

"But he hasn't got anything on!" said a little child.

"Good heavens! Just listen to the innocent child," said its father. And people whispered to each other, repeating what the child had said: "That little child says the emperor hasn't got anything on."

"Why, he hasn't got anything on!" the whole crowd was shouting at last, and the emperor's flesh crept, for it seemed to him that they were right.

"But all the same," he thought to himself, "I must go through with the procession." So he held himself even more proudly than before, and the lords-in-waiting walked on, bearing the train—the train that wasn't there at all!